Keeping
the Night
Watch

Keeping the Night Watch

HOPE ANITA SMITH

WITH ILLUSTRATIONS BY

E. B. LEWIS

Henry Holt and Company • New York

For Harold Keith Dorsey, Jr.
—H. A. S.

To my father, who is always there
—E. B. L.

Henry Holt and Company, LLC
Publishers since 1866
175 Fifth Avenue
New York, New York 10010
www.HenryHoltKids.com

Library of Congress Cataloging-in-Publication Data
Smith, Hope Anita.
Keeping the night watch / Hope Anita Smith ; with illustrations by E. B. Lewis.—1st ed.
p.   cm.
Summary: A thirteen-year-old African American boy chronicles what
happens to his family when his father, who temporarily left, returns home
and they all must deal with their feelings of anger, hope, abandonment, and fear.
ISBN-13: 978-0-8050-7202-0
ISBN-10: 0-8050-7202-0
[1. Family life—Fiction. 2. Fathers—Fiction. 3. African Americans—Fiction.]
I. Lewis, Earl B., ill. II. Title.
PZ7.S64934Ke 2008   [Fic]—dc22   2007012372

First edition—2008 / Designed by Laurent Linn
Printed in February 2009 in the United States of America by Worzalla, Stevens Point, Wisconsin, on
acid-free paper. ∞

3 5 7 9 10 8 6 4 2

Contents

FALL

Fall

We Are Family

The first one
is the hardest:
"family" dinner.
The prodigal son has returned.
Momma has killed the fatted calf,
cooked all of Daddy's
favorite foods.
The house smells
warm and safe—
as if Daddy never left.
We sit with pretend smiles
on our faces.
We are quiet and shy with each other.
Our eyes fixed on our plates
like we're watching
a really good TV show
and can't look away
for fear we might miss some action.
I move my food around on my plate,
but I don't eat.
I'm having "family" dinner with
a roomful of strangers.
My throat is so tight
not even Momma's candied yams
can squeeze through.

Daddy is full of compliments.

Only I know his words are plastic.

The kind that can't be recycled.

Byron remembers to say "please" and "thank you."

Zuri's so scared

she forgets she hates all vegetables and,

for the first time in her life,

cleans her plate.

After dinner, I wash dishes.

When Grandmomma comes in

to make a cup of tea, I say,

"This is a mess."

Grandmomma knows right away

I'm not talking about the dishes.

She hugs me and says,

"No, *this* is a family."

Family Cooking Instructions

Their conversation is sweet.
Their words are light and airy
like a just-baked cake.
They sugarcoat it
to cover up any flaws or imperfections.
Try to hide the sunken part.
They are so careful,
each wearing their own apron
to protect their clothed selves.
And that's why,
when I show up,
metal-cold and steel-gray,
they are not prepared.
I slice through
and we ooze out.
That's when we see that
we are not done in the middle.
We need to bake a little longer.

Pretending

Sometimes,
Zuri pretends that she is a lonely lady
who wants to get a dog
for company.
She makes me drive
on the imaginary trip to the pound.
"Look," she says,
"they're all wagging their tails.
They're all saying 'Take me.'
I'm going to pick the one who looks
like he needs me the most.
The one who licks my face and
loves me best.
That one," she says matter-of-factly,
pointing at a pillow on the couch.
Zuri is all smiles
as I chauffeur her "home."
But when I open the door for her
I see she's afraid.
She's eight,
and now she knows
that things can go wrong.
"What if—" she says,
and her eyes well up with tears.
She can't make her mouth form the words,
but I know what she's thinking.

What if her dog
leaves?
Just up and runs away.
Even though she does everything right.
Feeds it, loves it, gives it a nice place to sleep.
What if that's not enough?
"Hey," I say, trying to salvage
some of my baby sister's magic.
"This dog needs a name.
A name that will let him know
he belongs.
What do you think?"
And then I scratch the pillow dog
behind his ears and smile.
Zuri's face lights up and she smiles, too.
"I know," she says,
her face radiating belief.
"I'll name him Stay."

Sticks and Stones

Grandmomma always said,
"Be careful what you wish for . . ."
I didn't listen.
There were too many things to want.
Basketball camp,
my own room complete with TV and phone.
But I wished hardest
for Daddy to come back to us.
Come back to me.
Everything was changing,
my voice, my friends.
I needed Daddy.
Momma's love and Grandmomma's song
were warm and sweet,
but it wasn't enough.
Now Daddy's home
and my jaw is set.
My teeth are clenched.
My words are burrowing
deep down in my throat.
"You've never been scared
to ask anything," Momma says.
"Talk to your daddy."
But my questions are brick heavy.

I want to know:

Who are you?

What were you thinking?

Where did you go?

Why did you leave?

How could you do this to us?

These questions could bury him.

His answers could bury me.

"Talk to him," Momma says again.

"This could be a good thing."

"How?" I ask.

"Well," Momma says, smiling,

"what doesn't kill you,

will make you stronger."

Somebody's Callin' My Name

Daddy is standing in the middle of our driveway.

He bounces a basketball and sends

a coded message to my brother.

Byron hears the ball kiss the pavement and

is out of his room and out the door.

That won't work for me.

So Daddy calls my name.

"Hey, C.J., how about a little hoop?

You and Byron against the old man."

I pretend not to hear.

I let the breeze from the open window

blow his words away.

I crawl over to the window,

raise my periscope eyes up

over the windowsill.

Daddy and Byron play one-on-one.

Passing, shooting.

Daddy lets Byron steal the ball from him.

Byron scores.

Just like old times.

The only thing missing is me.

Daddy calls to me again.

"Hey, C.J.?"

I turn up my music.

I don't want to hear Daddy calling me.

His voice sounding like he never went away.

I lie on my bed,

close my eyes,

and pray,

"Oh, my Lord, oh, my Lord, what shall I do?"

Showdown at the O.K. Corral

When Daddy left,

our house was empty,

too big for the rest of us.

We couldn't fill up all the space.

Now that he's back,

I can't find a place to fit.

There isn't enough room for me.

Daddy looks the same,

but something's different.

He takes up too much space.

He's in my space.

His eyes are constantly

waving the white flag of surrender,

but I am like a gunfighter in the Old West.

I walk around with my words drawn,

ready to fire.

Because this house isn't big enough

for the two of us.

Family Tales

Every night it's always the same.

Twenty minutes of reading and then lights out.

Zuri knows the routine.

She picks a book and I read

while Zuri rests her head against my arm.

When I read, I am the prince with the slipper.

I am the prince who slays dragons

and awakens fair maidens

from their hundred-year-old sleep.

I am the prince who climbs a trellis of hair

to get to a beautiful girl trapped in a tower.

Even when I am reading about a spider

and a talking pig,

I am a prince—

to Zuri.

But tonight when I go to her room,

Zuri's not alone.

Daddy's there.

Zuri sits beside him,

looking like his most loyal subject.

"I picked out a book," she says.

"I'm ready to read," I answer as I make my way to her bed.

I am so focused on my goal

that I almost miss her next words:

"That's okay, C.J., I want Daddy to read to me."

My crown falls from my head
and her words cut,
each one a shard of glass.
"Care to join us?" Daddy asks as he opens the book.
"Can't," I say. "Lots of homework."
And then
I am gone.
I don't have time for Family Tales.

If You Can't Stand the Heat . . .

I am mad.

I am the worst kind of mad.

I don't yell.

I don't slam doors.

I don't throw things.

I'm a pot with the lid on,

I keep all my mad inside.

I just let it stew.

I want Byron to be mad, too,

but he isn't.

Says he doesn't want to hold on to mad.

He takes the lid off his pot,

lets mad go.

Says he wants his family back.

Says he's glad Daddy's home.

I'm mad at Daddy,

but it feels like I'm mad at Byron, too.

We're two different kinds of pots,

Byron and me,

and when it comes to Daddy,

we can't cook together.

Seven Ways of Looking at My Father

1. He is a shadow long and full, leaving little room for light and making it hard to see me.
2. He is a star that has burned out, lost his ability to be wished upon, but my family is light-years away from knowing this.
3. He is a fountain of happiness that can fill a cupful of people to overflowing: Momma, Zuri, Byron, Grandmomma, but not me. I have sprung a leak.
4. He is a table with a wobbly leg. It looks reliable but I wouldn't trust it with the good china.
5. He is the clock in the kitchen that never worked. His timing is all off. His true face is covered by his hands.
6. He is a mirage in the desert. A mighty tower you run toward for safety until you get to him and you realize he is just sand.
7. He is the messenger who brings the news but don't open the door—the news can't be good.

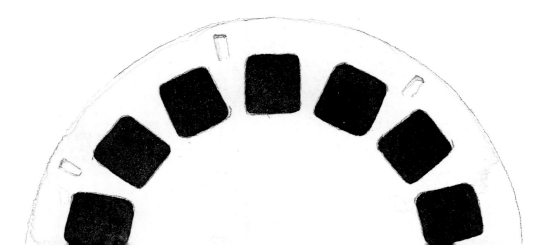

The Night Watchman

It's dark,

but I'm awake.

I'm making the rounds,

checking that everyone is safe.

This was Daddy's job before he left.

And even though he's back . . .

it's mine now.

My brother sleeps with one foot

hanging over the side of the bed.

Check.

I turn off Grandmomma's light and

quietly close her door.

Check.

My sister—

my sister isn't in her bed.

Her covers are pulled back

but she's not there.

The bathroom light is off.

She's not in my room.

I go to the kitchen.

Nothing.

And then I hear the soft sound of sleep.

I follow it into the living room and

there she is.

She has laid herself out in front of the door

like a welcome mat.

Zuri wakes as soon as I pick her up.

"Daddy!" she cries out, "don't go!"

"Shhh," I say, "it's me, C.J.

Go back to sleep."

"Where's Daddy?" Zuri asks.

"He's sleeping. Like you should be."

"I want to sleep here," she cries.

"You go back to bed," I say.

"I'll stand guard."

Zuri stops crying and is asleep again

before I return her to her room.

She believes me when

I say I'll stand guard.

And I will.

Because I am a man of my word.

It's what I've done

since my father came home.

I'm the night watchman.

Parents and Teachers

Zuri's teacher is worried
because she draws pictures of houses
that have no doors.
Her teacher sends home a note
addressed only to Momma,
as if Daddy is still
gone.
As if he couldn't be part of the solution.
The teacher wants a meeting.
She says it's to offer help.
She wants to deal with the problem head-on.
I know it's an accusation.
So she can point out
all the things our family's doing wrong.
I show the pictures to Grandmomma,
ask her what she thinks.
"Don't much matter what I think," she says.
"She's your sister.
What do you think?"
I say, "I'm not worried there are no doors.
I'll start worrying when there are no windows."

Unidentified Family Member (UFM)

My momma says
she doesn't recognize me.
I'm a stranger in my own house.
She says it looks like me,
but something's not right.
My eyes are dead.
My words are cold.
I stare at my face in the mirror,
but even I don't recognize me.
My heart hurts for my momma,
what she's missin'.
Her son.
Her "sweet baby boy."
And I hurt, too.
Who knew mad could make
me
disappear.

The Jeweler

I
can not
understand
how this black gem
who   is   my   father
could   just   stop   shining.
I   am   the   family   jeweler.
I   can   give   him   value,
praise and appraise him,
but   not   just   yet.
He must wait
for   me
now.

Sign Language

Our house is silent.
No one speaks in words.
We hold our thoughts and feelings hostage,
afraid of what they will do if we let them loose.
Instead,
Momma wears a painted-on smile that says
everything is okay, now.

My sister's hands latch on to Daddy

every chance they get.

They don't know how to be alone—

no, that's not true.

They know what it's like to be alone

and they say "we never want to be alone again."

Byron rocks,

imagining Daddy making his arms into a boat

and sailing him away to the land of dreams.

Byron's words arching

back and forth, back and forth.

They say, "Am I safe? Will you stay?"

I find new ways to avoid Daddy.

Can go the whole day without making eye contact.

When he asks a question

my shoulders say,

"I don't know. Beats me."

And Daddy's head is always bowed

like he's done something wrong

and he knows he's in trouble.

Listen.

Can you hear us?

We all talk at once

and our mouths never move.

A Talk on the Moon

Daddy made us all
sit outside with him and look up at
the moon.
"That," he said, "is a constant.
It's a sure thing.
And even though you don't believe it right now,
I'm a sure thing, too.
I'm as constant as the moon."
"The moon don't leave," Byron says.
"That's right," Daddy answers,
"the moon *doesn't* leave."
"But you did," Byron says in a huff.
"Let me tell you what happened,"
Daddy says.
"I had a problem that was just
a little bigger than me.
It was my black cloud.
It came and stood in front of me
and everything went black."
"Like an eclipse," I say.
"That's right," Daddy says.
"A total eclipse."
Zuri asks the question that
Byron and I can't voice:
"What's that mean, Daddy?"

"What it means," Daddy says
as he sits Zuri on his lap,
"is that I was there all the time,
but for a while,
you just couldn't see me."

Mountain Climbing

It takes
all of Daddy's energy to
move his words across the chasm
that separates us.
When he speaks, his words echo
and have lost all meaning when
they finally reach my ear.
I hope, one day,
that my snowy mountain of anger will be
so weighed down with Daddy's apology,
I will be overwhelmed
by an avalanche of forgiveness.

The Good Stuff

Byron says
sometimes he feels like
he's invisible.
Nobody can see him,
not even me.
People see me,
'cause I'm the oldest.
I even have Daddy's name,
Cameron James Washington III.
Everybody sees Zuri,
the baby,
the cute one.
Byron says he's in the middle,
wedged in between me and Zuri,
like a sandwich.
I say that makes him lucky.
He says, "Naw, man.
That makes you lucky.
Everybody knows
you can't make a sandwich
without bread."
"Maybe," I say, putting him in a headlock.
"but it wouldn't be much of a sandwich
without the stuff in the middle."

Crazy Glue

It holds fast.
Won't let go.
Clings to everything it touches,
nothing temporary about it.
It's forever.
Like the pain I feel
about what Daddy did.
My thoughts get stuck to
Leaving, Gone, and Left Behind.
Daddy's home, I remind myself.
Things are different now.
"Back to normal."
I want to believe this.
I want to stop hating my father.
That's not true.
I don't hate him.
I love him.
But I don't like him
much.
More than anything,
I want to let go,
but I can't.
I'm stuck.

Place Cards

I was summoned to the dining room.
Grandmomma wanted to talk to me.
"C.J.," she said,
"I used to love havin' people over
for dinner.
I'd cook all day long and make a fuss
puttin' out the 'gem of the first water' china and linens.
I'd set things out just so.
I used every ounce of good penmanship
from my school days to make
place cards for all my guests.
But every now and again,
somebody would decide they didn't want to
sit where I put them.
They'd take it upon themselves to sit
wherever they pleased.
Left-handed folks would wind up in
elbow fencing matches with right-handed folks.
Two people,
who had a fond dislike for each other,
would be forced to smile politely
as their hands touched
when they passed the dinner rolls.
It always caused a mess.

Here I had taken the time to write out
everyone's name
just so.
I wanted to make sure
a good time was had by all.
And just like that,
one misplaced person can knock everything
out of balance.
There's an order to everything, you know."
She scrawled something on a small
piece of white paper,
pursed her lips together, and looked at me
hard.
Her message was done.
What?
What was she saying to me?
Exasperated, I said,
"I don't get it, Grandmomma."
"Oh," she said, smiling,
"I believe you do."
She walked over to the table
and set a place card down
with my name on it and said,
"You, sit **here**."

Man-to-Man

Daddy and I are having a
"man-to-man" talk,
except I don't have anything to say.
"You don't have to talk," Daddy says,
"but you do have to listen.
When I was your age, I thought the
sun rose and set on my father.
Most days, it did.
But—"
I roll my eyes heavenward
and dare his words to defy the wall of
"I'm not listening."
Daddy pays no mind to my walls.
He lets out a long breath
and plows on.
He is determined.
As if the most important thing were
breaking through,
getting to the other side,
reaching
me.
"I made a mistake," he says.
"And for that, I couldn't be more sorry.

But I'm your daddy,

and I ain't gonna spend no more time

walking on eggshells

trying to win you over.

You're almost a man.

You got to make your own choices.

But for right now,

I'm gonna be the only man in this house.

Can't make you like me.

But what kind of father would I be

if I let you hang on to all that hate?

An angry black man

ain't no man at all.

You are my firstborn son.

You and Byron and Zuri are my light.

I'm here.

And I'm not going

nowhere,

no how,

no way."

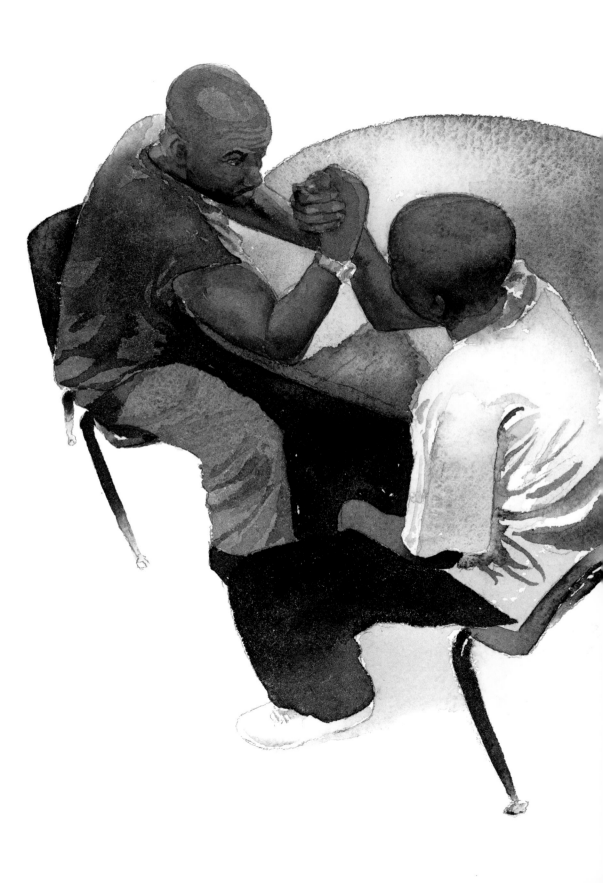

Spring

Maya's Sonnet

I didn't see her coming. Now she's here.
I hardly know where I should rest my eyes.
My words are all a jumble when she's near.
Now she's a thing with breasts and hips and thighs.

She smiles at me and I forget my name,
where I am, and how to move my feet.
But Preacher says my heart's to blame.
I think love's cruel but also very sweet.
She calls me "Cameron" and I respond,
but to all others I am still C.J.
Her voice is like a fairy's magic wand;
she only has to speak and I'll obey.

My happy and my sad are all a swirl.
My heart has been abducted by a girl.

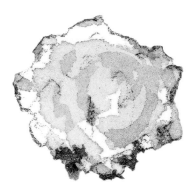

Preacher's Sermon
on the Mount

Today
Preacher's eyes are ablaze
and his words are rock hard.
"Police
ain't even tryin' to protect me.
All I have to do is stand
downwind of a crime scene
and I'm 'suspect.'
I'm 'every black man.'
When something goes down,
cops come up and block my way,
trying to keep me out.
'You live around here?' they ask.
I say, 'Yes, sir.'
And they say, 'Don't get smart, boy.'
So, I stare at the ground,
try to become the nobody
they think I am.
In art, they told us that black was
the absence of all color, but,
man, black is the absence of everything."
Preacher is beside me yet he's
far away when he says,
"It would be so easy to stuff myself

into the box they designed for Brothas of Color,
but I ain't goin' out like that.
I got a 4.0 GPA,
and when I graduate,
I'm bound for the Promised Land.
Morehouse College."
Preacher laughs when he adds,
"And even they have to admit,
I am one fine brotha!
What's that song your grandmomma
is always singing?
'Ain't Gonna Let Nobody Turn Me 'Round'?"
I smile because
Grandmomma's voice reaches even here,
and all I can say is
Amen.

Tongue-Tied

One digit

dialing

seven digits.

That's all it takes to

make my voice

reach across the miles.

The receiver is my fortress.

Behind it, I can say anything.

My words walk with a sure step.

They are cocky,

strut across the telephone lines,

and never look down.

Until Maya picks up.

Then the first word stops,

abruptly,

getting caught in my throat.

And every word that comes after

plows into the one in front of it.

Fifty-two-word pile up.

Right smack dab

in the middle of

our conversation.

Field Trip

The permission slip only required

one parent's signature.

Piece of cake.

I handed it to Momma.

But Momma said, "I'm busy.

Get your daddy to sign it."

I really wanted to go,

but I couldn't see asking *him*.

"I'll wait," I said.

I stood my ground.

Pen and paper outstretched to Momma.

"When's the trip?" she asked.

"Next Friday."

"Well, then, you'll be waitin' a month of Sundays

for me to sign it.

I told you, C.J., I'm busy."

Momma pointed at the paper and said,

"It says here: Parent's signature.

You've got two.

I'm not the only one with a pen."

Daddy was in the other room.

I wasn't sure how much he'd heard.

I didn't care.

I couldn't back down now. Could I?

I'd skip the trip.

Miss out sitting next to Maya on the
two-hour bus ride.
Spend the day doing "busy work"
in the library.
I looked down at the permission slip
dangling from my fingertips,
holding on to it for dear life,
and then I looked toward the room
where Daddy was.
My feet couldn't move.
My pride wouldn't let them.
"Looks like you're stuck between a rock
and a hard spot," Momma said as she walked
out of the room, dismissing herself,
thereby dismissing me.

Fences

I don't know how it happened.

One minute Preacher and I

are on the same side of the fence,

the next, the fence is between us.

"How's about shootin' some hoop?" Preacher asked.

I paused.

I *wanted* to walk Maya home.

I *needed* to study.

I said nothing.

"My bad," Preacher says.

"You got to check with Momma *and* Maya.

You need a unaminous vote.

You are whipped, man—without a belt!"

And then it was my turn:

"Those who ain't got, preach. Amen?"

Preacher is silent.

"You don't have to say amen," I say,

"it's the truth anyhow."

And there it was.

Offense. Defense. Our fence.

It wouldn't separate us forever,

but it had done its job for today.

Lunch Is a Battlefield

Lunch is probably the worst subject
you have to take in school.
Every day you run the gauntlet
and try to come out on the other side
alive.
It helps if you've got a sidekick,
but today I'm solo.
Preacher is MIA.
"You're on your own, soldier," he says,
slapping me on the back and heading off
to parts unknown (to me).
I grab my tray and make a break
for an empty seat across the room.
I focus.
I keep my eyes on the prize,
making sure to avoid the land mines
of bored junior jocks looking for
new prey to prey upon.
And the outcasts looking hopeful
as you approach,
but my eyes say it all.
They say,
"I can't afford the guilt by association stigma
of being seen with you."

Nothing personal, but

I have to watch my step.

One wrong move and I bite the lunchroom news bullet.

The little one that goes in clean and explodes on impact.

I won't even know how bad I've been hit

until someone comes up and puts his hand

through my midsection,

literally.

It's a slow death,

and even worse,

it doesn't last forever.

The bell will ring and all casualties

will return to classrooms

until tomorrow

when I can do it again.

An opportunity

to die another day.

Row, Row, Row . . .

This is the best worst day of my life.
I am walking Maya home.
My hands are sweaty, my mouth is dry,
and every sermon I ever heard at
Preacher's Church of How to Get a Girl
is forgotten.
I reach for conversation,
but what I really want to say
sits up on the highest shelf.
My heart is racing, but I slow down my feet.
I need to make this last . . .
until I get it right.
Time is my ladder
and every minute adds a rung.
Maya's mouth has not stopped moving
since we left school.
Her words are skinny-dipping
in the Lake of Conversation.
Carefree and easy.
No fear of being naked.
It looks like Preacher was right;
"girls have wicked serious skills
when it comes to us (boys)."
But then I notice something.
You'd miss it if you weren't looking
at just the right angle, in just the right light.

She is wearing a sparkling crown of perspiration
right at her hairline.
And she is fidgeting with her fingers.
That's when I know, as Grandmomma would say,
we are in the same boat.
We just have different ways of rowing.

For Real

This ain't no game, this love is really real.
'Cause talk is cheap if nothing's ever said.
Step up and tell her how you really feel.

Grandmomma says, "With love, you don't conceal.
No point in hiding horses in the shed."
This ain't no game, this love is really real.

Preacher claims I'm a thief because I steal
glances at her and store them in my head.
Step up, and tell her how you really feel.

If I'm not careful I'm afraid that she'll
be first to make tracks where I dare not tread.
This ain't no game, this love is really real.

Sometimes I think my heart is made of steel.
If she shot me down, then all I'd be is dead.
Step up, and tell her how you really feel.

No *Price Is Right* or *Let's Make a Deal*.
No changing the channels on fear and dread.
Step up! And tell her how you really feel.

(Nick) Tuck

I stare into the mirror
and I see a face.
My face looking back at me.
I put my hand to my face,
let my fingers travel across the
terrain that is my skin.
They confirm what I
already know to be true.
This road is too rough,
no one will travel it—
it needs to be smoothed out.
I am God
making mountains of shaving cream
in the palms of hands.
I bring the mountains to the Muhammad
that is my face,
spreading it evenly over the surface.
I open the razor, place a new blade inside
and twist it closed.
Preacher says your first shave should be done
manually
without the help of electricity.
It's a rite of passage, he says.
You can't take any shortcuts.

I turn my head slightly and guide the razor down
my face.
I look at the road I have just made and see
that it is good.
I smile as I begin the descent again, this is *nick* easy.
Wait until Maya *nick* sees me,
the *nick* new me.
The razor trembles in my hand *nick*.
I wipe the perspiration from my brow.
And so it goes *nick* for *nick* some *nick* time
until the road is *nick* smooth.

I tear off pieces of toilet paper

the way Preacher showed me,

the way Daddy did when Byron and I stood watching,

and placed them on each of the little nicks on my face.

I stare into the mirror

and I see what looks like a million red dots silhouetted

by a halo of toilet paper.

"It might look pretty bad," Preacher warned,

"but it's the end product we're going for."

I open the door and head to my room.

I pass Grandmomma in the hallway.

Grandmomma lifts my chin with her hand and

turns my head to the right and to the left and says,

"Mmph, mmph, mmph."

"What?" I ask defensively.

"I just think it's sad, that's all."

"What's sad?" I ask.

"All this blood and you missed the little bit of peach fuzz

you were trying to get rid of!"

Best-Kept Secret

I wanted to give Maya
something.
Let her know that she was
my girl.
Momma said flowers.
Grandmomma said every girl needed
her very own monogrammed lace handkerchief.
I went over to Preacher's and asked him
what he thought.
"I got just the thing for you, man," Preacher says.
He pulls a thin pink box from under his bed.
"I was saving this for when I get a girl, but
since I'm on hiatus, it's all yours."
Preacher plopped the box down in my lap.
I undid the black ribbon, lifted the lid,
and peeked under the tissue paper.
My eyes nearly popped out of my head.
"It's lingerie," Preacher announced,
a little too loudly for me.
"Shhhhhhhhhh!" I whispered,
sure that the whole house had heard.
"Aw, man," Preacher said, grabbing the
contents from the box.
"Preacher!" I yelled.
"Don't hold them up for
God and all the world to see!"

"Come on, C.J., ain't nobody here but you and me."
Preacher made sure that I left with that little pink box.
I took it home.
Shoved it under my bed.
It was destined to be
Victoria's best-kept secret—
at least until Preacher came off hiatus.
Tomorrow I would get Maya what every girl needs:
her very own monogrammed lace handkerchief.

Can You Hear Me Now?

I have learned to walk on little cat feet

around my house.

It allows me to

be

with Daddy

without him knowing it.

Today I hear his voice through the

partially opened door to Byron's room.

I lean into the wall and listen.

Allow myself to actually hear what he is saying.

"A woman can bring a man down

faster than any fist.

Your momma wound up and gave me a punch that

struck me in the heart and I was down for the count.

I still haven't recovered!"

I smiled.

Byron was silent.

He's too young for this, I thought to myself.

"You're still a little young for this," Daddy said.

"You won't understand everything I'm tellin' you,

but forewarned is forearmed.

All you really need to know is:

You're a good man.

You're a gentleman.

And even when you haven't got a dime to your name

you've got your courtesy.

Hold on to it like it's gold

'cause it is.

A lady deserves respect.

Open the door for her.

Help her on with her coat.

Don't take nothing that ain't bein' offered.

And remember, makin' a baby don't make you a man.

You just keep what I'm tellin' you under your hat.

No need for all this now.

Bein' in love is a beautiful thing.

I don't want you to miss a minute of it.

If she's anything like your momma,

you'll be all right."

Daddy opened the door and walked out.

I waited a minute or two to go into

Byron's room.

He and Daddy had had

a true man-to-man talk.

No, it was a heart-to-heart talk,

and I found myself wishing

I was Byron.

"Hey, Byron," I said pushing the door open.

But there was no one there.

Basketball practice, that's where he was.

Every day until five p.m.

So who was Daddy talking to?

I looked out into the hall

and saw Grandmomma staring back at me.

My eyes were full of questions,

but my mouth couldn't move.

Grandmomma just smiled and said,

"There's more than one way to skin a cat."

Zuri's ABCs

All of the family got one,

Byron, Mama, Daddy, Grandmomma, and me. Our names

Carefully penned in Crayola Candy Apple Red.

Daddy cried the hardest, and that's to be

Expected.

Fathers, who leave, keep paying even when they come back.

Grandmomma sits sagelike,

Holding the letter to her chest,

Imitating the Virgin Mary, as if the Baby were

Jesus,

King of kings.

"Lord, have

Mercy" were the only words she spoke. The letter said:

Now that Daddy's back, let's not be scared,

Okay?

Parents are good when there are two.

Quiet houses are

Really

Scary.

Time to love each other again.

Until forever. And that means a

Very long time.

With

XXXs and OOOs

Yours,

Zuri

Light at the End of the Tunnel

I am his son.
I could deny it, but why?
I have his eyes, his mouth, his hands,
his heart.
Not literally, but
there are times when I hear the beat.
The thump, thump of
Let go.
Walk out.
Good-bye.
It's easy on the ear.
The feet want to keep time.
"What you have to remember,"
Daddy says, "is that each step takes you
a-way."
It's not something I could have learned
on my own.
I have to learn from someone
who's been there.
Daddy's smile says,
"I do what I can."
Daddy is trying.
He is still jobless,
but he wants to bring
something to me,
Byron, Zuri, Mama,
and Grandmomma.

We are all tired of stumbling around
in the dark of uncertainty.
He wants to give us light.
He wants to be our sun
rising.

Blueprint

When the quake hit,

it hit hard,

shook us to our core.

Our fine bone-china security

fell to the floor and shattered.

Emotions were strewn about

and still we just kept

stepping over, around, and on them.

Now Daddy is home

and the aftershocks are keeping

us all on alert.

Our earthquake kit is always

close at hand.

It contains all we need

so that disappointment won't

catch us off guard.

"Fool me once, shame on you.

Fool me twice . . ."

I search my family's faces

trying to figure out why

they're not afraid.

"You know the answer," Grandmomma says.

"You just don't know you know."

She smiles and I smile back because I do know.

I know this:

The original floor plan for our family

is sound.

In spite of everything,

our foundation is firm.

Our house is still standing.

Dance with Me

Byron turns on the music.
An "old school" song fills the house.
He shuts his eyes and lets the
tornado of sound catch him up in its
whirlwind.
Zuri closes her book and smiles big.
She doesn't need an invitation.
She is already there.
Grandmomma comes into the room
with her brow furrowed,
shaking her head from side to side.
"Jump back!" she shouts. "Let an old lady
show you how it's really done!"
Grandmomma becomes the melody;
and Byron and Zuri, her perfect harmony.
And then I hear a POP!
It is my father snapping his fingers to the beat.
He James Brown's his way out onto the
dance floor.
Momma comes in full of parental authority,
but before she can speak
Daddy swoops her into his arms and
her protests are carried away on quarter notes.
Here is my family and they are dancing.

They dance to free themselves from their fears.

They dance to exorcise their sadness.

They dance to celebrate the ties that bind.

I watch them.

And then I feel the pull of the moon

drawing me to them.

I go over and tap Daddy on the shoulder.

Our eyes meet and his smile is frozen.

He cannot read my face.

"I'd like to cut in," I say.

Daddy steps back,

offers me my mother's hand.

I make my move.

I take Daddy's hand and I start to dance

with him

around the room.

We all laugh

hard

and the water that falls from our eyes

flows into one big river,

but we are not afraid.

We are like Peter on the Sea of Glass,

only we don't fall in.

We keep our eyes on Him.

We dance on our tears.